J PB
Gantos, Jack.
Rotten Ralph´s show and tel
Boston : Houghton Mifflin,
c1989.

New pocket 5-13-04 Rs

09
/

ROTTEN RALPH'S SHOW and TELL

Written by Jack Gantos

Illustrated by Nicole Rubel

Houghton Mifflin Company   Boston

To my family – N.R.

To Seth – J.G.

Library of Congress Cataloging-in-Publication Data

Gantos, Jack.
    Rotten Ralph's show and tell/written by Jack Gantos and
illustrated by Nicole Rubel.
        p.   cm.
    Summary: Sarah takes her rotten cat Ralph to school for Show and
Tell and he behaves terribly, as usual, by spoiling everyone's show.
    ISBN 0-395-44312-1
    [1. Cats—Fiction. 2. Behavior—Fiction. 3. Schools—Fiction.]
I. Rubel, Nicole, ill. II. Title.
PZ7.G15334Rol   1989   89-30911
[E]—dc19   CIP
PAP ISBN 0-395-60285-8   AC

The character of Rotten Ralph was originally created by
Jack Gantos and Nicole Rubel.

Printed in the United States of America

WOZ 10 9 8 7 6 5 4 3

Ralph is Sarah's rotten cat but Sarah loves him
anyway.

One morning Sarah went to take her violin to school
for Show and Tell. But Rotten Ralph had broken
the strings.

"Ralph," said Sarah, "I wish you wouldn't be
so rotten."

William Tell

And when she went to get her stamp collection,
Rotten Ralph had licked the stamps and pasted
them all over himself.

"Ralph!" cried Sarah. "Now I have nothing to take
to school."

Then she said, "Ralph, I'll have to take you. But you must promise to be good and remember your ABC's so you can write them for the class."

"I promise," Ralph thought to himself.

On the school bus Sarah was very proud of Ralph.
He kept his hands to himself. He didn't stick out his
tongue. And he didn't trip anyone with his tail, even
though he wanted to.

"Oh, Ralph," said Sarah. "We'll be sure to win first
prize."

When Show and Tell started, the teacher called on one of Sarah's friends.

"This is my red ant farm," she said. But before she could finish, Ralph knocked over the ant farm and all the red ants escaped.

"Don't be so rotten, Ralph," whispered Sarah. "And think of your ABC's."

"This is my favorite home movie," said another
student.

But when he turned on the projector, Rotten Ralph
made frightening hand shadows on the screen.

"When the teacher calls on me, Ralph," said Sarah,
"I want you to behave."

Next a student took them outside to show off his
prize pumpkin. But Rotten Ralph put it on his head
and chased everyone around.

Finally it was Sarah's turn. She walked Ralph to the front of the classroom. "This is my smart cat, Ralph," she said. "He knows how to write his ABC's." But Ralph only wanted to be rotten. He beat the erasers together and covered everyone with chalk dust.

Then he scratched his claws across the blackboard
until everyone's ears hurt.
"Please, please behave yourself, Ralph," cried Sarah,
"or we won't win first prize."

Sarah's teacher was upset.

"I'm going to give you one more chance," he said.

"Now go sit in the back of the class and write your ABC's."

But when Rotten Ralph tried, he got them all
mixed up.
So he rang the school bell before it was time to
go home.

"The only prize your cat has won is the dunce cap," said Sarah's teacher. And he made Ralph sit all alone during lunch break.

After school Sarah decided to walk home.

On the way Ralph felt bad for not winning. He knew
that he was as smart as everyone else.

"It's okay if you can't do your ABC's," said Sarah.

"I still love you anyway."

When they got home, Sarah made him his favorite cake.

But Ralph wasn't hungry. Instead, he wrote his ABC's into the icing on the cake.

Then he jumped up onto Sarah's lap and she pasted
a big gold star on his nose.
"Oh, Ralph," said Sarah. "You're smart enough
for me."